PIGGIE BEAR'S
Power of Happiness

MARA JAMES
Illustrated By MATTHEW MEW

BROWN BOOKS KIDS

Piggie Bear's Power of Happiness

Brown Books Kids
Dallas / New York
www.BrownBooksKids.com
(972) 381-0009

A New Era in Publishing®

Publisher's Cataloging-In-Publication Data

Names: James, Mara, author. | Mew, Matt, illustrator.
Title: Piggie Bear's power of happiness / Mara James ; illustrated by Matthew Mew.
Other Titles: Power of happiness
Description: Dallas ; New York : Brown Books Kids, [2022] | Series: [Piggie Bear] ; [2] | Interest age level:
    003-005. | Summary: "By teaching young children to identify their emotions, release extra energy, and
    perform deep belly breathing and self-hugs, Piggie Bear is there to encourage kids through every feeling"--
    Provided by publisher.
Identifiers: ISBN 9781612545592 (hardcover)
Subjects: LCSH: Emotions--Juvenile fiction. | Stuffed animals (Toys)--Juvenile fiction. | Breathing exercises--
    Juvenile fiction. | CYAC: Emotions--Fiction. | Stuffed animals (Toys)--Fiction. | Breathing exercises--Fiction.
Classification: LCC PZ7.1.J38536 Pi 2022 | DDC [E]--dc23

This book has been officially leveled by using the F&P Text Level Gradient™ Leveling System.

ISBN 978-1-61254-559-2
LCCN 2021922623

Printed in the United States
10 9 8 7 6 5 4 3 2 1

For more information or to contact the author, please go to
www.ELFempowers.org.

Piggie Bear® is owned by the Extraordinary Lives Foundation, a 501(c)(3)
whose mission is to improve children's mental health & wellness.

Dedication

This book is dedicated to the memory of
Blaze Bernstein and all those who do not have
the opportunity to live long, happy lives.
May their memory be a blessing.

Acknowledgments

We are so grateful for the families, friends, donors, and sponsors who have helped us share Piggie Bear with children around the world. The Extraordinary Lives Foundation has grown tremendously because of your support, and we thank you from the bottom of our hearts to the tips of our toes. You are amazing!

It's so nice to meet you.
I am excited that you will be
joining me at my school today.
This is my teacher, Ms. Brown.

Good morning, class!

One of my favorite feelings is HAPPINESS.

When I am happy, I feel full of love and joy.

I smile from EAR ⌣to⌣ EAR.

What makes you feel happy?

Blaze, can you please share with us what makes you happy?

Friends, did you know that there are some times when you may not feel happy?

Sometimes you may feel sad, angry, or scared.

SAD

ALL FEELINGS ARE IMPORTANT.

ANGRY

SCARED

Aa Bb Cc Dd Ee Ff Gg Hh Ii Jj Kk Ll

There are times when I feel ANGRY. Matt, what makes you feel angry?

"I feel angry
when my brother
pulls a toy out
of my hand,"
Matt says.

Friends, when you feel angry,
it can help to move your body.

You can *RUN* in place or do
JUMPING jacks to release energy.

Then, it can help to practice my
favorite Piggie Bear breathing.

Breathe in through your nose and feel your belly grow BIGGER.

Next, breathe out through your mouth and feel your belly get SMALLER.

Let's do this a few more times. Do you notice you feel more relaxed?

"I feel sad when I am not able to play with my friends," Loulie says.

That would make me feel sad, too. When you feel sad, give yourself a **BIG PIGGIE BEAR HUG** to help you feel better.

Let's all give ourselves a BIG Piggie Bear hug.
Wrap your arms around your shoulders
and give yourself a big squeeze.

AHHHH . . . doesn't that feel good?

"I felt scared when I was asked a question and I didn't know the answer," Rozzie says.

When you feel scared, it can help to move your body, and then practice your Piggie Bear breathing.

In our classroom, Ms. Brown has created a quiet space. You can use this space to help you get to know your feelings. You can create a quiet space anywhere. Where is your favorite place to go for quiet time?

"My bed is my favorite place to go for quiet time," Blaze says.

Rozzie the frog says, "I like to take a bath."

"I like to go on a walk outdoors," Loulie says.

Matt the gorilla says, "I don't have a favorite place to go when I need quiet time."

During quiet time, you may notice that your heart has many feelings. Sometimes when I feel angry, sad, or scared, I play my favorite Water the Flower game to help my heart feel happier.

Let's play it together now!

Close your eyes and imagine a flower in your heart. Now, imagine rain falling down from the sky. See the rain watering the flower in your heart.

GREAT JOB!

Watch as your flower grows **BIGGER** and **BIGGER**. Then, watch the water wash away your unhappy feelings. See the water go into the ground. Now, look at the flower in the middle of your heart. See it shining **BIG** and **BRIGHT**.

Thank you, Piggie Bear, for sharing with us today about feelings. I love the Water the Flower game. It is a great way to feel happy any time.

About the Author

Mara James is the founder of the Extraordinary Lives Foundation (ELF), a 501(c)(3) tax-exempt organization dedicated to improving the mental health and well-being of children.

Mara created the character Piggie Bear® as a therapeutic tool to increase children's social-emotional learning, which has a direct and positive impact on their mental health and well-being. Piggie Bear empowers children and teaches them self-care techniques for dealing effectively with their emotions.

Mara is a strong advocate for mental health awareness. She lives in Orange County, California, and holds positions on various mental health committees in Southern California. At the time of this printing, Mara was elected to a significant position on the Orange County Behavioral Health Advisory Board. She is also part of the Council for the Advancement of Research in Global Mental Health at Columbia University.

About the Illustrator

Matthew Mew has been working with children's books and materials as an author and illustrator for over thirty-five years. After graduating from UCLA with a degree in design, he worked for six years as a character illustrator in the Disneyland Creative Services Department. For the past thirty years he has been a freelancer, designing and illustrating children's products and print media for companies both large and small.